BIG GOOF and LITTLE GOOF

A Pet for the Goofs • A Change of Seasons • Bigger and Smaller

by Joanna and Philip Cole   illustrated by M.K. Brown

SCHOLASTIC INC.

New York

TO
Rachel
—J.&P.C.

FOR
Madeleine
— M.K.B.

Library of Congress Cataloging-in-Publication Data

Cole, Joanna.
Big Goof and Little Goof / by Joanna and Philip Cole; illustrated
by M. K. Brown.

p.   cm.
Summary: Follows the amusing misadventures of two foolish friends.
ISBN 0-590-41591-3
[1. Friendship—Fiction. 2. Humorous stories.] I. Cole, Philip
(Philip A.) II. Brown, M.K. (Mary K.), ill. III. Title.
PZ7.C67346Bi 1989
[E]—dc19   88-31130
                                      CIP
                                       AC

12 11 10 9 8 7 6 5 4   0 1 2 3 4/9
                                           36
Printed in U.S.A.

First Scholastic printing, September 1989

A PET FOR THE GOOFS

Big Goof and Little Goof lived together.
Sometimes they got everything all mixed up.
They were pretty goofy.

One day Big Goof and Little Goof were working in the yard when a turtle walked by.

"Look at that cute little animal!" said Little Goof. "What is it?"

"I don't know," said Big Goof.

"We could keep it for a pet," said Little Goof.

"We never had a pet before," said Big Goof. "We might do something wrong."

"We will read a book and learn how to take care of it," said Little Goof.

The Goofs picked up the turtle and walked to the library.

"Do you have a book on pets?" Big Goof asked.

The librarian showed the Goofs a whole shelf of books about pets. Big Goof picked one out. It was called OUR FRIEND THE DOG.

"*Dogs have four feet*," read Big Goof.

"One, two, three, four," counted Little Goof. "Our pet has four feet. He is a dog!"

"*When a dog is happy, it wags its tail*," read Big Goof.

"Our dog has a tail, but he is not wagging it. He must be sad," said Little Goof.

Big Goof read on, "*A dog needs a bone to chew and a collar to wear.*"
"No wonder our dog is sad," said Little Goof. "He doesn't have those things."
"Let's go get them right now," said Big Goof.
"Come on, Doggie," said Little Goof.

But the bone did not make Doggie wag his tail.
Neither did the collar. The Goofs felt terrible.

Their pet was not happy.
They walked around their yard wondering what to do.

When they passed the pond, Doggie jumped in and swam around.
As he swam, his tail moved back and forth.

"Look at his tail!"
cried Big Goof.

"He must be
a water dog,"
said Little Goof.
"He is happy
when he is
swimming."

Now when the weather is nice, the Goofs take their dog for a swim in the pond. When it is too cold or rainy to go out, Doggie swims in the bathtub.

"We learned something, Little Goof," said Big Goof.

"Books don't tell you everything. You have to find out some things for yourself."

One summer evening, Little Goof wanted to draw.
But he could not find any paper. He tore some pages
off the calendar and drew pictures on the back of them.

The next morning Big Goof looked at the calendar.

"It is winter already!" he said. "How time flies!"

Big Goof got ready to go out. He put on his warm coat. He put on his warm hat and his scarf and mittens.

He got his ice skates and opened the door.
Just then Little Goof woke up.

"Wait for me!" he cried.
"I love to go ice skating."

Little Goof put on his warm clothes, too.
He got his skates. The two Goofs walked down to the pond.
Doggie was swimming happily.

"The ice is very soft this year. It will not be easy to skate," said Big Goof.

"We could go swimming instead,"
said Little Goof.

"Won't we be cold?"
said Big Goof.

"You have to be brave,"
said Little Goof.
"Don't be a chicken."

The Goofs were very brave. They took off their winter clothes and jumped in. They swam for a long time. It was fun!

Then they went inside.
"We could catch cold swimming in December," said Big Goof.
So they had hot chocolate and sat by the fire to warm up.

"It is one thing to be brave," Big Goof said,
"but we must not be foolish."

BIGGER AND SMALLER

One night, Big Goof and Little Goof were watching TV.

The TV lady said, "If you do not get enough sleep, you will get sick."

"Oh, no!" said Big Goof. "Look how late it is!"

"We'd better go to bed right away!" said Little Goof.

The two Goofs were in a big hurry. They took off their shoes.
They took off their pants. They took off their shirts.
They threw their clothes all over the place.

Then they jumped into bed and went right to sleep.

Very early the next morning, while it was still dark,
a car honked outside. The two Goofs woke up.
They were so sleepy, they could hardly open their eyes.
They found clothes and began to put them on.

Big Goof looked down.

"I must be getting
bigger!" he cried.
"I am too big for
my clothes."

"Look at *me!*" cried Little Goof.
"I am getting *smaller!*
I am too small
for my clothes!"

"This is terrible,"
said Big Goof.
"I was *already*
big."

"And I was already little," said Little Goof.

"I will be too big to sit in my chair," said Big Goof.
"I will be too little to sit in mine," said Little Goof.

"I will be too big to fit in the bathtub," said Big Goof.

"I will be so little I might go down the drain," said Little Goof.

"We will be dirty from never taking a bath!"

"That TV lady was right," Big Goof said.
"We did not get enough sleep, and we got sick."

"I got Getting-Bigger sickness!"
said Big Goof.

"I got Getting-Smaller sickness!"
said Little Goof.

"If we are sick,
we ought to be
in bed."

Slowly, slowly, the two Goofs took off their shoes.
They took off their pants. They took off their shirts.
They folded their clothes neatly, got into bed,
and went to sleep.

Later that same morning, when the sun was shining brightly, a car honked outside. The Goofs woke up.
This time they were not sleepy. Their eyes were wide open.
They put on their clothes the right way.

"Look what happened!" said Little Goof.

"That TV lady was sure smart. All that sleep made us the right size again," said Big Goof.

Just look at those Goofs now.
Isn't it wonderful to see them all better and back to normal?